THE WONDERFUL WIZARD OF OZ

VOL. 4

ADAPTED FROM THE NOVEL BY L. FRANK BAUM

Writer: ERIC SHANOWER
Artist: SKOTTIE YOUNG
Colorist: JEAN-FRANCOIS BEAULIEU
Letterer: JEFF ECKLEBERRY

Assistant Editors: LAUREN SANKOVITCH & LAUREN HENRY
Associate Editor: NATE COSBY
Senior Editor: RALPH MACCHIO

Special Thanks to Chris Allo, Rich Ginter, Jeff Suter & Jim Nausedas
Collection Editor: MARK D. BEAZLEY
Assistant Editors: NELSON RIBEIRO & ALEX STARBUCK
Editor, Special Projects: JENNIFER GRÜNWALD
Senior Editor, Special Projects: JEFF YOUNGQUIST
SVP of Print & Digital Publishing Sales: DAVID GABRIEL
Production: JERRY KALINOWSKI
Book Design: SPRING HOTELING

Editor in Chief: AXEL ALONSO
Chief Creative Officer: JOE QUESADA
Publisher: DAN BUCKLEY
Executive Producer: ALAN FINE

visit us at www.abdopublishing.com

Reinforced library bound edition published in 2014 by Spotlight, a division of the ABDO Group, PO Box 398166, Minneapolis, Minnesota 55439. Spotlight produces high-quality reinforced library bound editions for schools and libraries. Published by agreement with Marvel Characters, Inc.

Printed in the United States of America, North Mankato, Minnesota.
102013
012014
This book contains at least 10% recycled materials.

Marvel.com
© 2014 Marvel

Library of Congress Cataloging-in-Publication Data

Shanower, Eric.
  The wonderful Wizard of Oz / adapted from the novel by L. Frank Baum ; writer: Eric Shanower ; artist: Skottie Young. -- Reinforced library bound edition.
     pages cm
  "Marvel."
  Summary: An eight-volume, graphic novel adaptation of L. Frank Baum's tales of Dorothy, a little girl from Kansas who is blown by a storm to the magical land of Oz, where she has amazing adventures while trying to get home.
  ISBN 978-1-61479-226-0 (vol. 1) -- ISBN 978-1-61479-227-7 (vol. 2) -- ISBN 978-1-61479-228-4 (vol. 3) -- ISBN 978-1-61479-229-1 (vol. 4) -- ISBN 978-1-61479-230-7 (vol. 5) -- ISBN 978-1-61479-231-4 (vol. 6) -- ISBN 978-1-61479-232-1 (vol. 7) -- ISBN 978-1-61479-233-8 (vol. 8)
  1. Graphic novels. [1. Graphic novels. 2. Fantasy.] I. Young, Skottie, illustrator. II. Baum, L. Frank (Lyman Frank), 1856-1919. III. Title.
  PZ7.7.S453Won 2014
  741.5'973--dc23
                    2013029128

All Spotlight books are reinforced library binding
and manufactured in the United States of America.

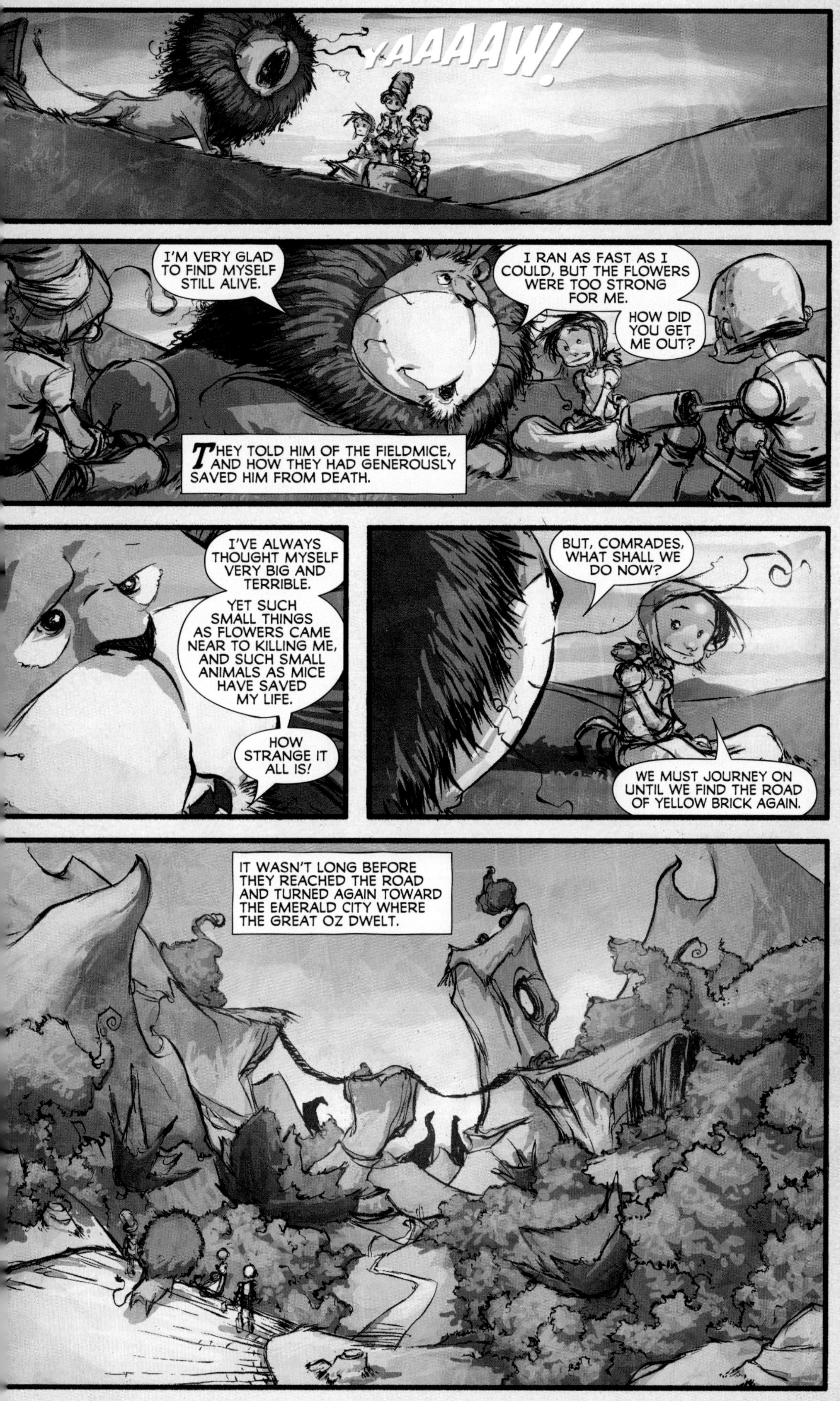
YAAAAW!
I'M VERY GLAD TO FIND MYSELF STILL ALIVE.
I RAN AS FAST AS I COULD, BUT THE FLOWERS WERE TOO STRONG FOR ME.
HOW DID YOU GET ME OUT?
THEY TOLD HIM OF THE FIELDMICE, AND HOW THEY HAD GENEROUSLY SAVED HIM FROM DEATH.
I'VE ALWAYS THOUGHT MYSELF VERY BIG AND TERRIBLE.
YET SUCH SMALL THINGS AS FLOWERS CAME NEAR TO KILLING ME, AND SUCH SMALL ANIMALS AS MICE HAVE SAVED MY LIFE.
HOW STRANGE IT ALL IS!
BUT, COMRADES, WHAT SHALL WE DO NOW?
WE MUST JOURNEY ON UNTIL WE FIND THE ROAD OF YELLOW BRICK AGAIN.
IT WASN'T LONG BEFORE THEY REACHED THE ROAD AND TURNED AGAIN TOWARD THE EMERALD CITY WHERE THE GREAT OZ DWELT.

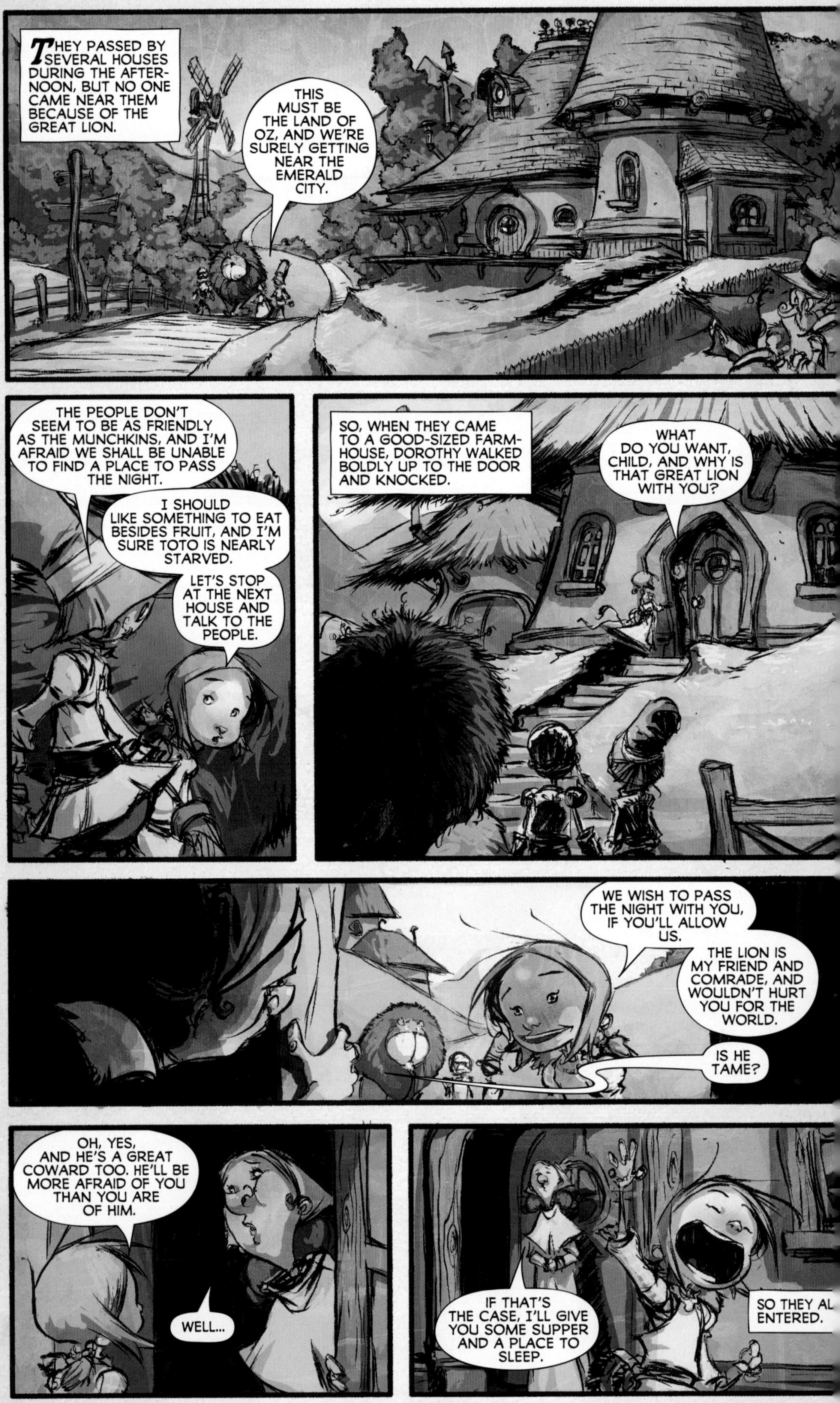
THEY PASSED BY SEVERAL HOUSES DURING THE AFTERNOON, BUT NO ONE CAME NEAR THEM BECAUSE OF THE GREAT LION.
THIS MUST BE THE LAND OF OZ, AND WE'RE SURELY GETTING NEAR THE EMERALD CITY.
THE PEOPLE DON'T SEEM TO BE AS FRIENDLY AS THE MUNCHKINS, AND I'M AFRAID WE SHALL BE UNABLE TO FIND A PLACE TO PASS THE NIGHT.
I SHOULD LIKE SOMETHING TO EAT BESIDES FRUIT, AND I'M SURE TOTO IS NEARLY STARVED.
LET'S STOP AT THE NEXT HOUSE AND TALK TO THE PEOPLE.
SO, WHEN THEY CAME TO A GOOD-SIZED FARMHOUSE, DOROTHY WALKED BOLDLY UP TO THE DOOR AND KNOCKED.
WHAT DO YOU WANT, CHILD, AND WHY IS THAT GREAT LION WITH YOU?
WE WISH TO PASS THE NIGHT WITH YOU, IF YOU'LL ALLOW US.
THE LION IS MY FRIEND AND COMRADE, AND WOULDN'T HURT YOU FOR THE WORLD.
IS HE TAME?
OH, YES, AND HE'S A GREAT COWARD TOO. HE'LL BE MORE AFRAID OF YOU THAN YOU ARE OF HIM.
WELL...
IF THAT'S THE CASE, I'LL GIVE YOU SOME SUPPER AND A PLACE TO SLEEP.
SO THEY AL ENTERED.

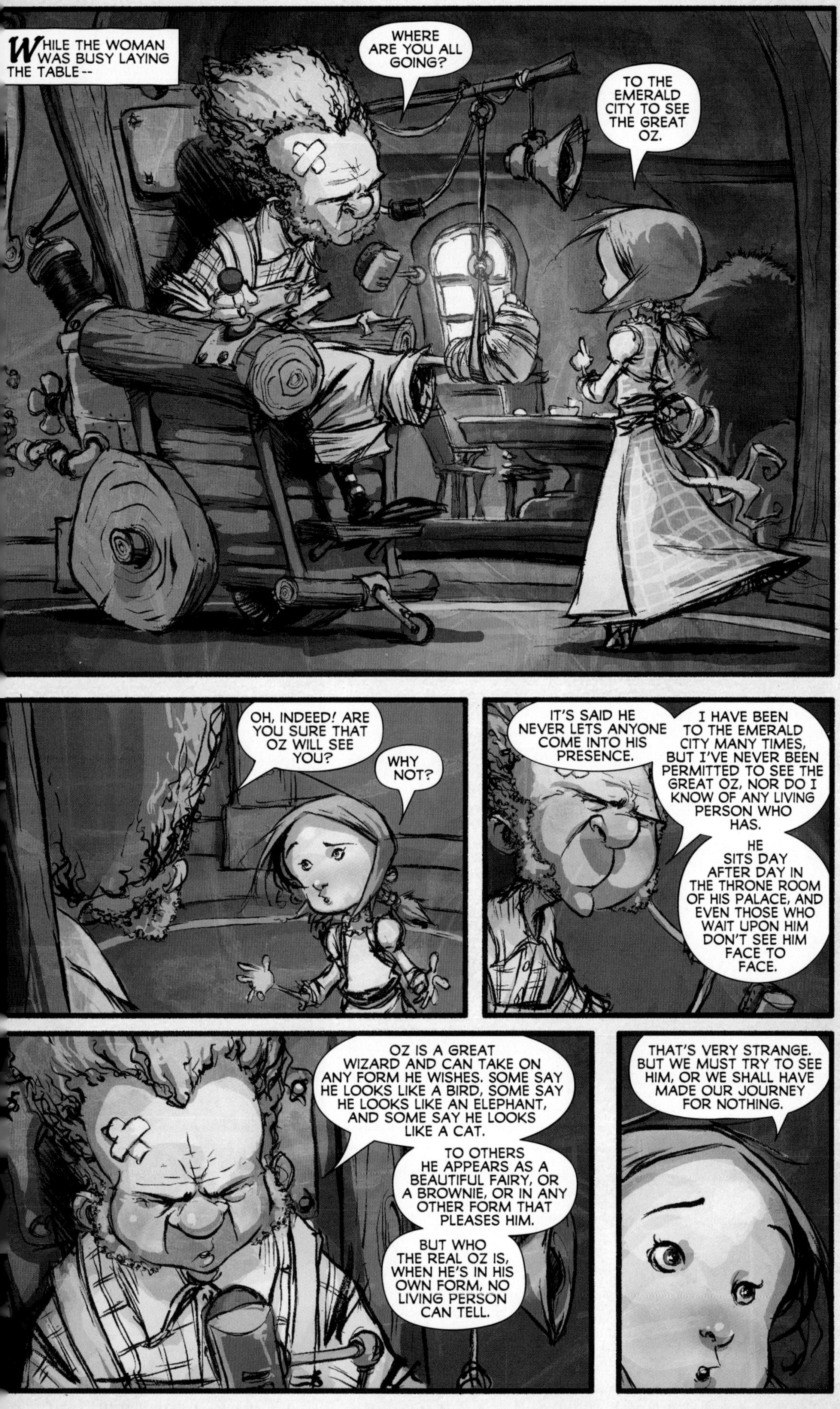
WHILE THE WOMAN WAS BUSY LAYING THE TABLE--
WHERE ARE YOU ALL GOING?
TO THE EMERALD CITY TO SEE THE GREAT OZ.
OH, INDEED! ARE YOU SURE THAT OZ WILL SEE YOU?
WHY NOT?
IT'S SAID HE NEVER LETS ANYONE COME INTO HIS PRESENCE.
I HAVE BEEN TO THE EMERALD CITY MANY TIMES, BUT I'VE NEVER BEEN PERMITTED TO SEE THE GREAT OZ, NOR DO I KNOW OF ANY LIVING PERSON WHO HAS.
HE SITS DAY AFTER DAY IN THE THRONE ROOM OF HIS PALACE, AND EVEN THOSE WHO WAIT UPON HIM DON'T SEE HIM FACE TO FACE.
OZ IS A GREAT WIZARD AND CAN TAKE ON ANY FORM HE WISHES. SOME SAY HE LOOKS LIKE A BIRD, SOME SAY HE LOOKS LIKE AN ELEPHANT, AND SOME SAY HE LOOKS LIKE A CAT.
TO OTHERS HE APPEARS AS A BEAUTIFUL FAIRY, OR A BROWNIE, OR IN ANY OTHER FORM THAT PLEASES HIM.
BUT WHO THE REAL OZ IS, WHEN HE'S IN HIS OWN FORM, NO LIVING PERSON CAN TELL.
THAT'S VERY STRANGE. BUT WE MUST TRY TO SEE HIM, OR WE SHALL HAVE MADE OUR JOURNEY FOR NOTHING.

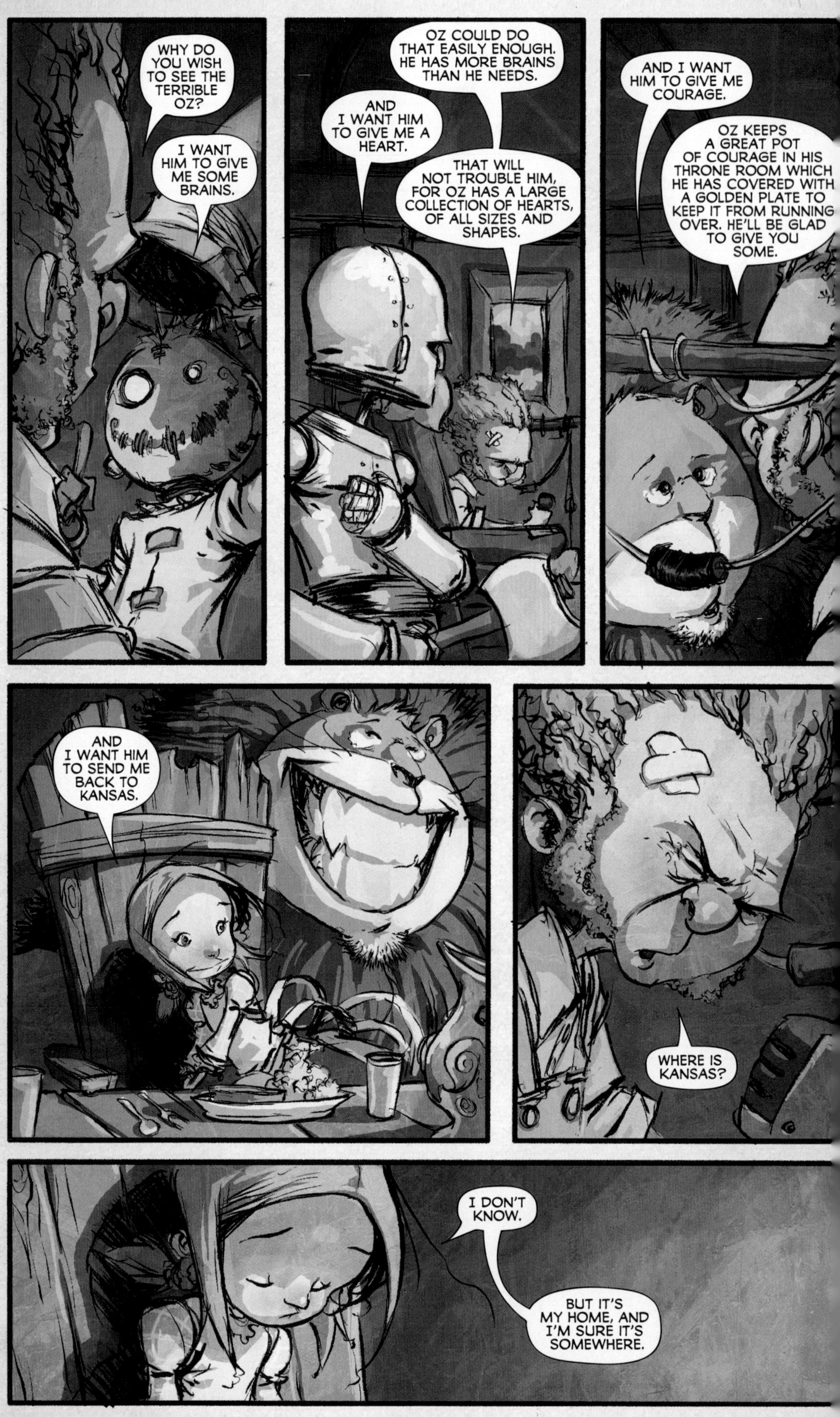
WHY DO YOU WISH TO SEE THE TERRIBLE OZ?
I WANT HIM TO GIVE ME SOME BRAINS.
OZ COULD DO THAT EASILY ENOUGH. HE HAS MORE BRAINS THAN HE NEEDS.
AND I WANT HIM TO GIVE ME A HEART.
THAT WILL NOT TROUBLE HIM, FOR OZ HAS A LARGE COLLECTION OF HEARTS, OF ALL SIZES AND SHAPES.
AND I WANT HIM TO GIVE ME COURAGE.
OZ KEEPS A GREAT POT OF COURAGE IN HIS THRONE ROOM WHICH HE HAS COVERED WITH A GOLDEN PLATE TO KEEP IT FROM RUNNING OVER. HE'LL BE GLAD TO GIVE YOU SOME.
AND I WANT HIM TO SEND ME BACK TO KANSAS.
WHERE IS KANSAS?
I DON'T KNOW.
BUT IT'S MY HOME, AND I'M SURE IT'S SOMEWHERE.

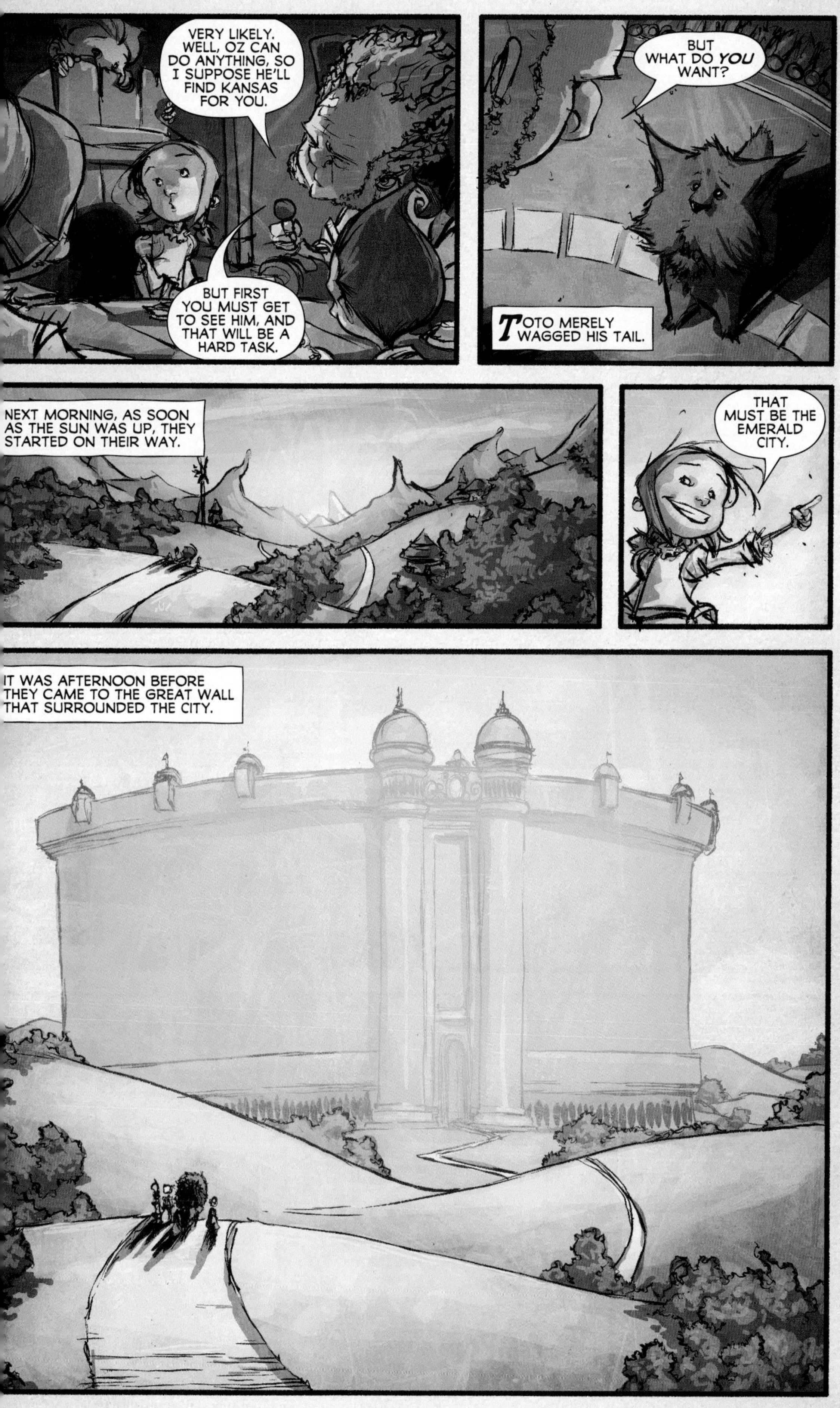
VERY LIKELY. WELL, OZ CAN DO ANYTHING, SO I SUPPOSE HE'LL FIND KANSAS FOR YOU.
BUT FIRST YOU MUST GET TO SEE HIM, AND THAT WILL BE A HARD TASK.
BUT WHAT DO *YOU* WANT?
TOTO MERELY WAGGED HIS TAIL.
NEXT MORNING, AS SOON AS THE SUN WAS UP, THEY STARTED ON THEIR WAY.
THAT MUST BE THE EMERALD CITY.
IT WAS AFTERNOON BEFORE THEY CAME TO THE GREAT WALL THAT SURROUNDED THE CITY.

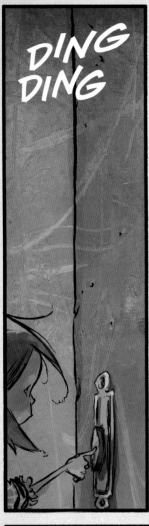

DING
DING

WHAT DO YOU WISH IN THE EMERALD CITY?

WE CAME HERE TO SEE THE GREAT OZ.

IT HAS BEEN MANY YEARS SINCE ANYONE ASKED ME TO SEE OZ.

HE'S POWERFUL AND TERRIBLE. IF YO COME ON AN IDLE C FOOLISH ERRAND T BOTHER THE WISE REFLECTIONS OF TH GREAT WIZARD, HE MIGHT BE ANGRY AND DESTROY YOU ALL IN AN INSTANT.

IT'S NOT A FOOLISH ERRAND, NOR AN IDLE ONE. IT'S IMPORTANT, AND WE'VE BEEN TOLD THAT OZ IS A GOOD WIZARD.

SO HE IS, AND HE RULES THE EMERALD CITY WISELY AND WELL.

BUT TO THOSE WHO ARE NOT HONEST, OR WHO APPROACH HIM FROM CURIOSITY, HE'S MOST TERRIBLE.

FEW HAVE EVER DARED ASK TO SEE HIS FACE.

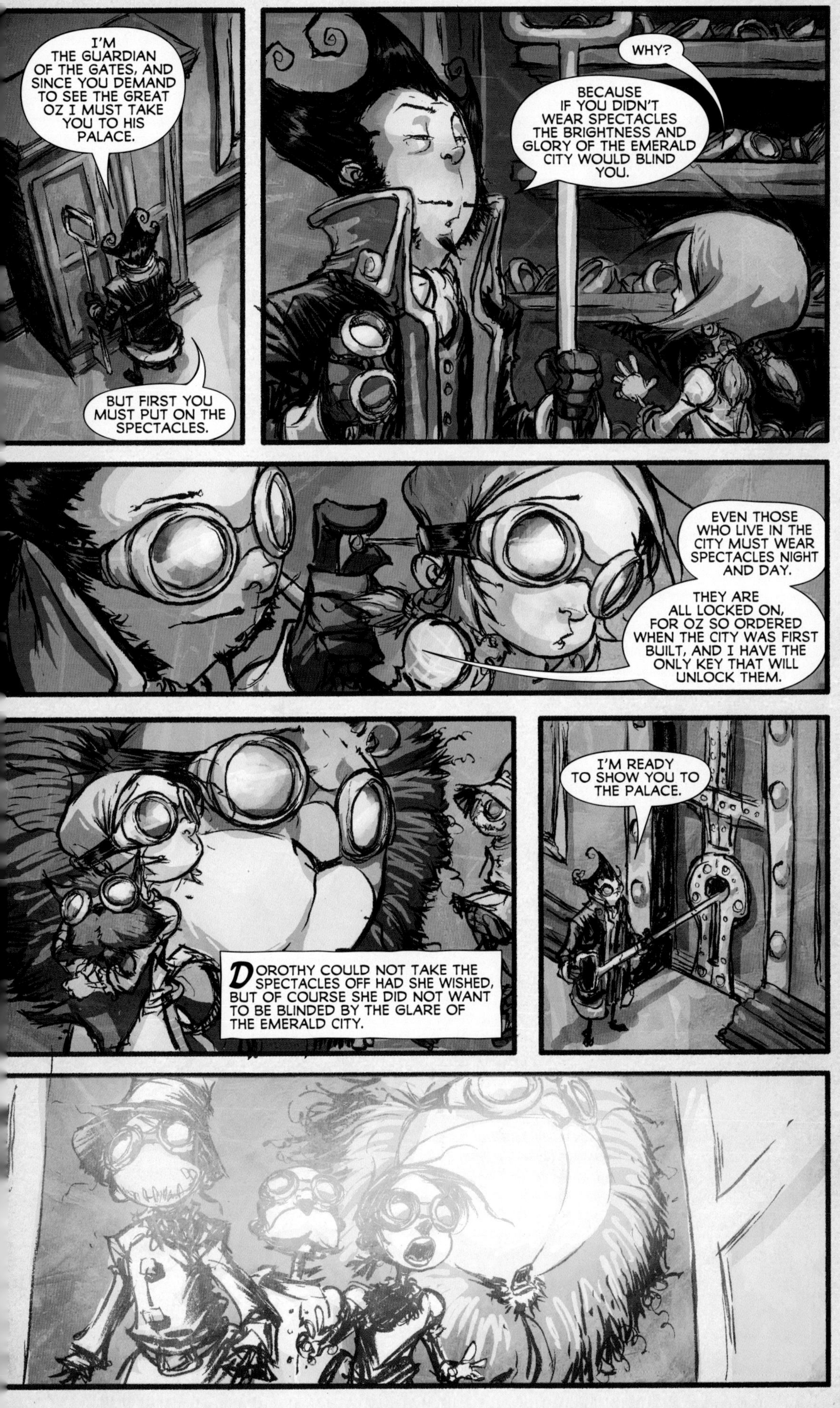
I'M THE GUARDIAN OF THE GATES, AND SINCE YOU DEMAND TO SEE THE GREAT OZ I MUST TAKE YOU TO HIS PALACE.
BUT FIRST YOU MUST PUT ON THE SPECTACLES.
WHY?
BECAUSE IF YOU DIDN'T WEAR SPECTACLES THE BRIGHTNESS AND GLORY OF THE EMERALD CITY WOULD BLIND YOU.
EVEN THOSE WHO LIVE IN THE CITY MUST WEAR SPECTACLES NIGHT AND DAY.
THEY ARE ALL LOCKED ON, FOR OZ SO ORDERED WHEN THE CITY WAS FIRST BUILT, AND I HAVE THE ONLY KEY THAT WILL UNLOCK THEM.
DOROTHY COULD NOT TAKE THE SPECTACLES OFF HAD SHE WISHED, BUT OF COURSE SHE DID NOT WANT TO BE BLINDED BY THE GLARE OF THE EMERALD CITY.
I'M READY TO SHOW YOU TO THE PALACE.

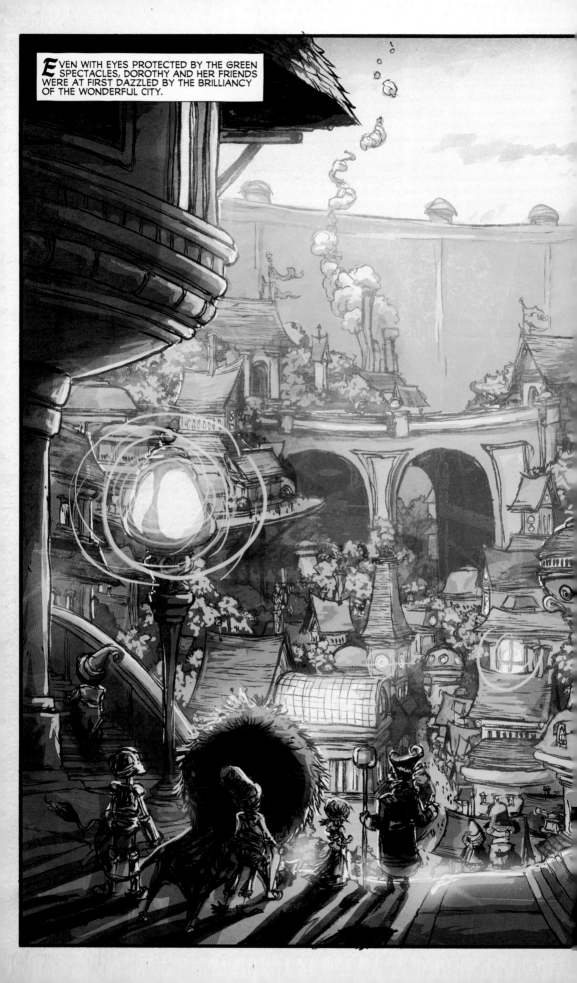

EVEN WITH EYES PROTECTED BY THE GREEN SPECTACLES, DOROTHY AND HER FRIENDS WERE AT FIRST DAZZLED BY THE BRILLIANCY OF THE WONDERFUL CITY.

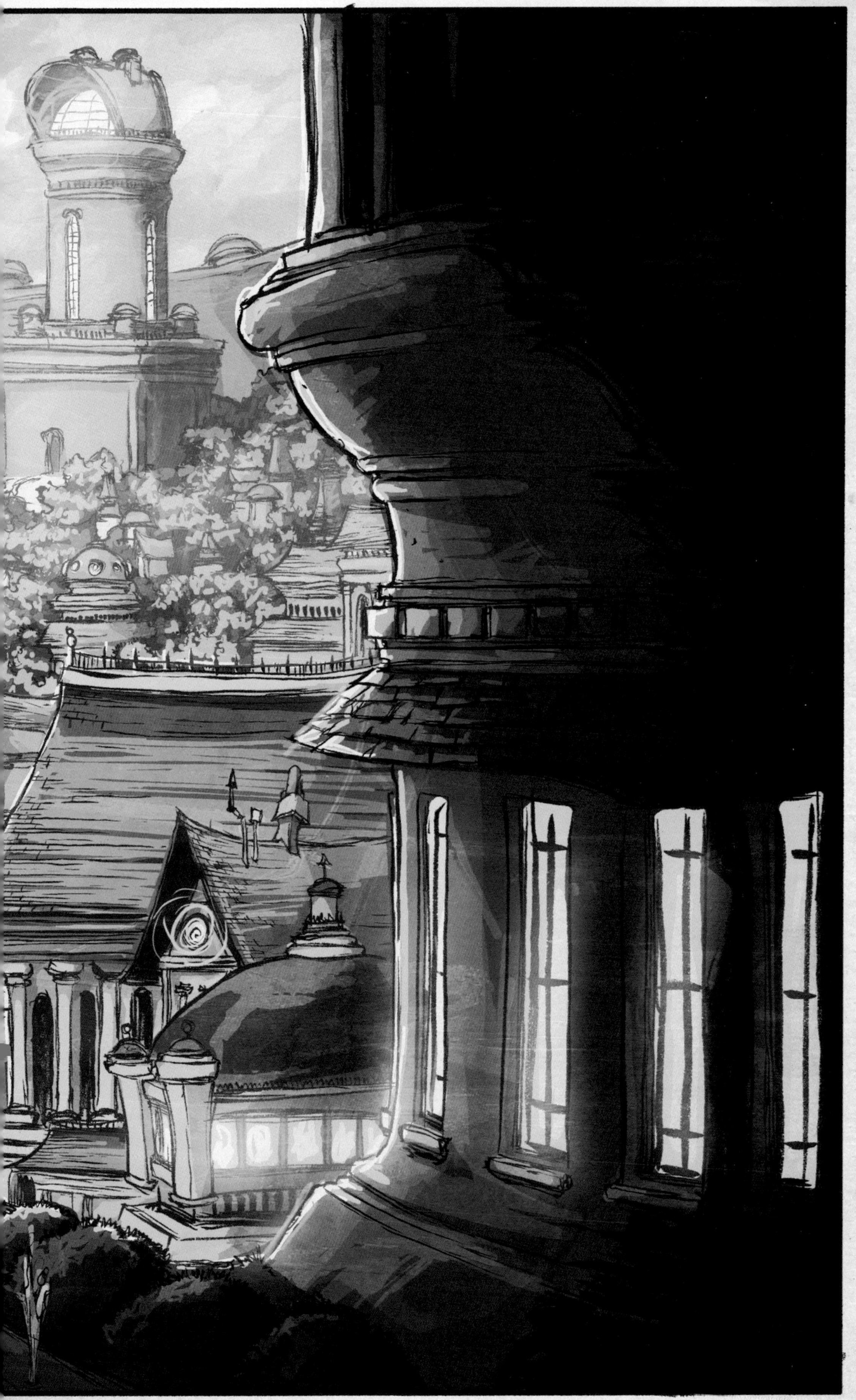

THERE WERE MANY PEOPLE WALKING ABOUT. EVERYONE SEEMED HAPPY AND CONTENTED AND PROSPEROUS.

THEY LOOKED AT DOROTHY AND HER COMPANY WITH WONDERING EYES -- AND THE CHILDREN ALL RAN AWAY WHEN THEY SAW THE LION -- BUT NO ONE SPOKE TO THEM.

THE GUARDIAN OF THE GATES LED THEM THROUGH THE STREETS UNTIL THEY CAME TO A BIG BUILDING, EXACTLY IN THE MIDDLE OF THE CITY, WHICH WAS THE PALACE OF OZ, THE GREAT WIZARD.

HERE ARE STRANGERS, AND THEY DEMAND TO SEE THE GREAT OZ.

STEP INSIDE AND I WILL CARRY YOU MESSAGE TO HIM.

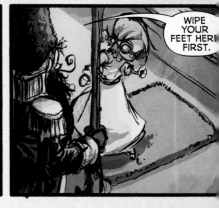

WIPE YOUR FEET HERE FIRST.

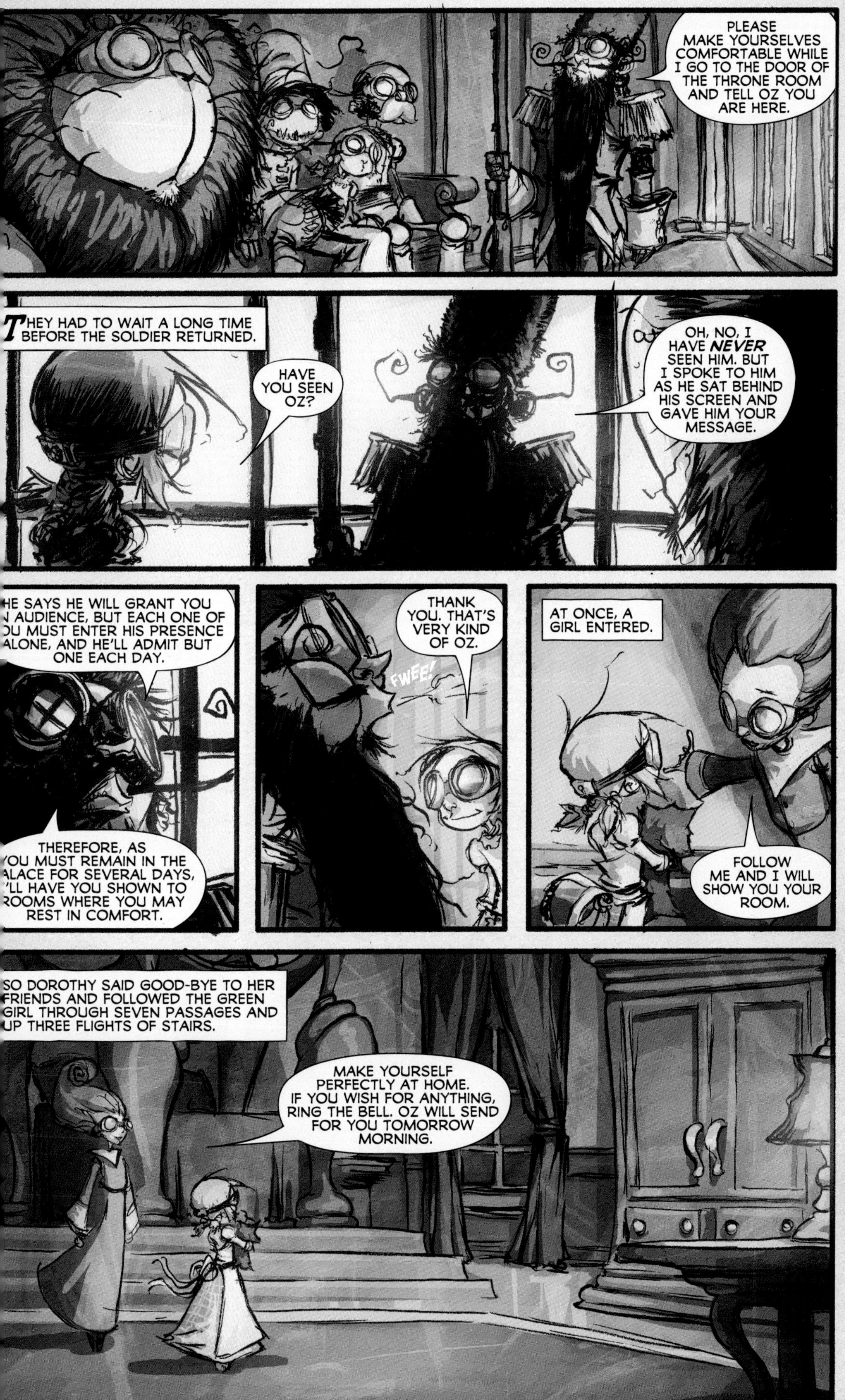
PLEASE MAKE YOURSELVES COMFORTABLE WHILE I GO TO THE DOOR OF THE THRONE ROOM AND TELL OZ YOU ARE HERE.
THEY HAD TO WAIT A LONG TIME BEFORE THE SOLDIER RETURNED.
HAVE YOU SEEN OZ?
OH, NO, I HAVE NEVER SEEN HIM. BUT I SPOKE TO HIM AS HE SAT BEHIND HIS SCREEN AND GAVE HIM YOUR MESSAGE.
HE SAYS HE WILL GRANT YOU AN AUDIENCE, BUT EACH ONE OF YOU MUST ENTER HIS PRESENCE ALONE, AND HE'LL ADMIT BUT ONE EACH DAY.
THEREFORE, AS YOU MUST REMAIN IN THE PALACE FOR SEVERAL DAYS, I'LL HAVE YOU SHOWN TO ROOMS WHERE YOU MAY REST IN COMFORT.
THANK YOU. THAT'S VERY KIND OF OZ.
FWEE!
AT ONCE, A GIRL ENTERED.
FOLLOW ME AND I WILL SHOW YOU YOUR ROOM.
SO DOROTHY SAID GOOD-BYE TO HER FRIENDS AND FOLLOWED THE GREEN GIRL THROUGH SEVEN PASSAGES AND UP THREE FLIGHTS OF STAIRS.
MAKE YOURSELF PERFECTLY AT HOME. IF YOU WISH FOR ANYTHING, RING THE BELL. OZ WILL SEND FOR YOU TOMORROW MORNING.

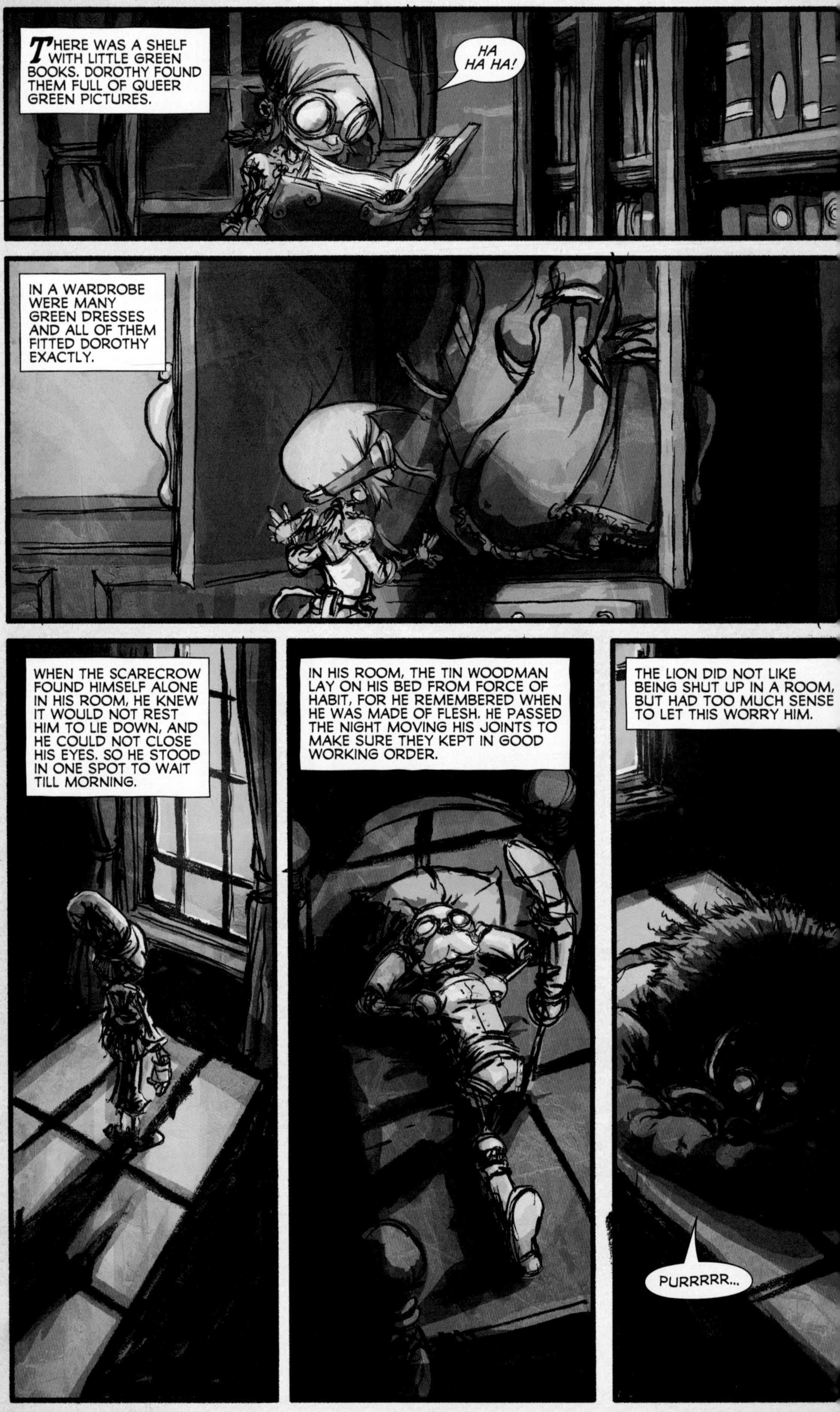
THERE WAS A SHELF WITH LITTLE GREEN BOOKS. DOROTHY FOUND THEM FULL OF QUEER GREEN PICTURES.
HA HA HA!
IN A WARDROBE WERE MANY GREEN DRESSES AND ALL OF THEM FITTED DOROTHY EXACTLY.
WHEN THE SCARECROW FOUND HIMSELF ALONE IN HIS ROOM, HE KNEW IT WOULD NOT REST HIM TO LIE DOWN, AND HE COULD NOT CLOSE HIS EYES. SO HE STOOD IN ONE SPOT TO WAIT TILL MORNING.
IN HIS ROOM, THE TIN WOODMAN LAY ON HIS BED FROM FORCE OF HABIT, FOR HE REMEMBERED WHEN HE WAS MADE OF FLESH. HE PASSED THE NIGHT MOVING HIS JOINTS TO MAKE SURE THEY KEPT IN GOOD WORKING ORDER.
THE LION DID NOT LIKE BEING SHUT UP IN A ROOM, BUT HAD TOO MUCH SENSE TO LET THIS WORRY HIM.
PURRRRR...

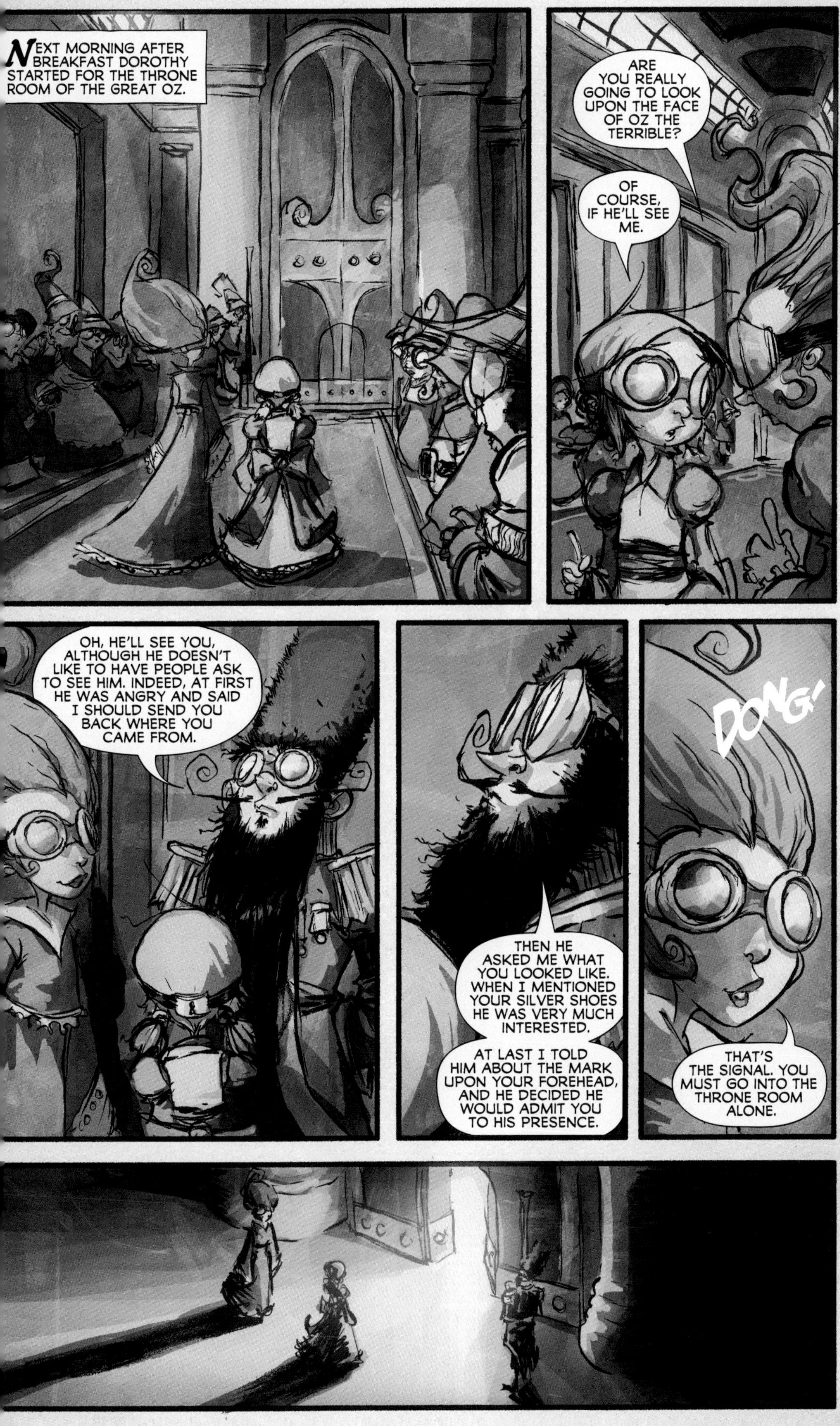
NEXT MORNING AFTER BREAKFAST DOROTHY STARTED FOR THE THRONE ROOM OF THE GREAT OZ.
ARE YOU REALLY GOING TO LOOK UPON THE FACE OF OZ THE TERRIBLE?
OF COURSE, IF HE'LL SEE ME.
OH, HE'LL SEE YOU, ALTHOUGH HE DOESN'T LIKE TO HAVE PEOPLE ASK TO SEE HIM. INDEED, AT FIRST HE WAS ANGRY AND SAID I SHOULD SEND YOU BACK WHERE YOU CAME FROM.
THEN HE ASKED ME WHAT YOU LOOKED LIKE. WHEN I MENTIONED YOUR SILVER SHOES HE WAS VERY MUCH INTERESTED.
AT LAST I TOLD HIM ABOUT THE MARK UPON YOUR FOREHEAD, AND HE DECIDED HE WOULD ADMIT YOU TO HIS PRESENCE.
DONG!
THAT'S THE SIGNAL. YOU MUST GO INTO THE THRONE ROOM ALONE.

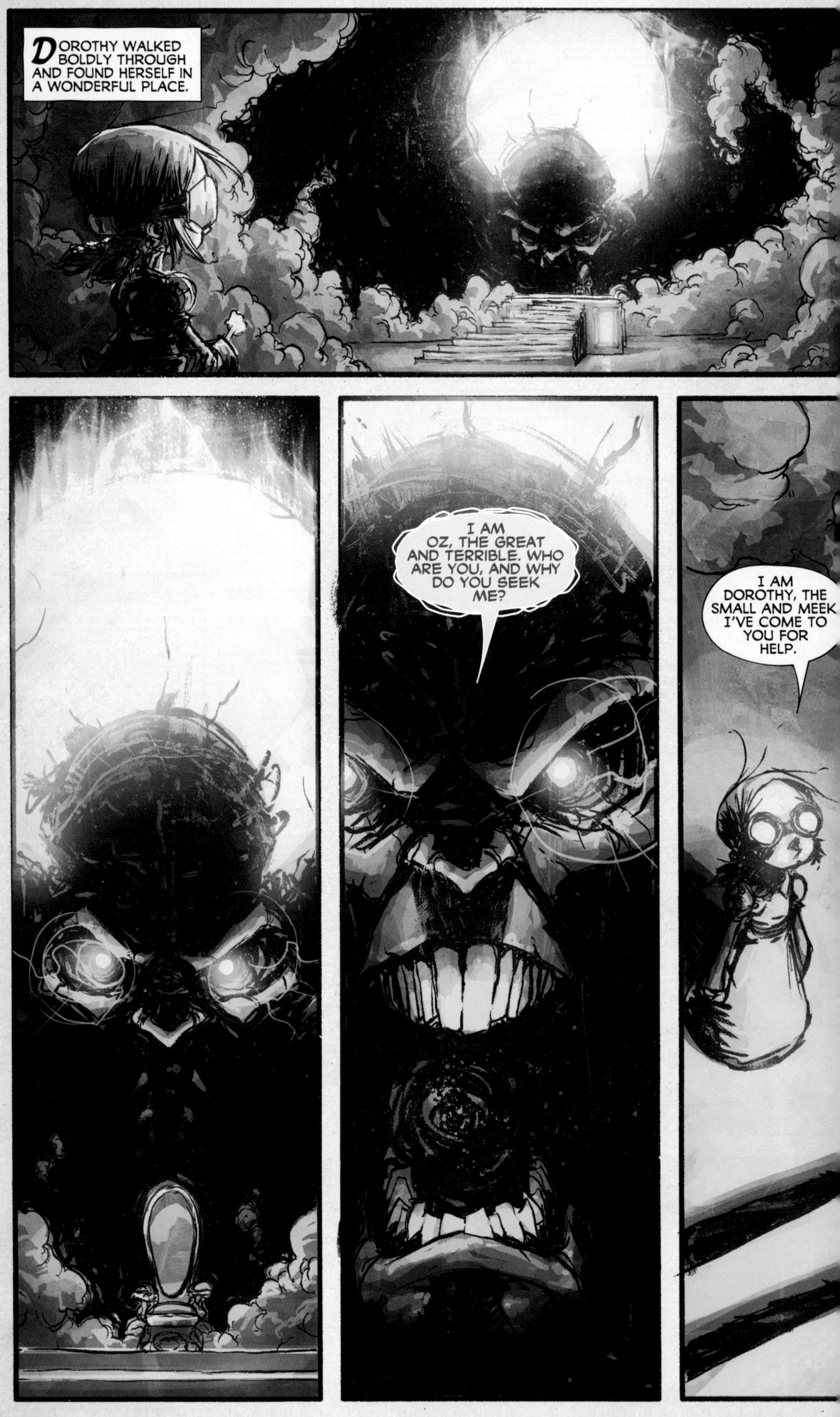
DOROTHY WALKED BOLDLY THROUGH AND FOUND HERSELF IN A WONDERFUL PLACE.
I AM OZ, THE GREAT AND TERRIBLE. WHO ARE YOU, AND WHY DO YOU SEEK ME?
I AM DOROTHY, THE SMALL AND MEEK I'VE COME TO YOU FOR HELP.

WHERE DID YOU GET THE SILVER SHOES?
I GOT THEM FROM THE WICKED WITCH OF THE EAST WHEN MY HOUSE FELL ON HER AND KILLED HER.
WHERE DID YOU GET THE MARK UPON YOUR FORE-HEAD?
THAT'S WHERE THE GOOD WITCH OF THE NORTH KISSED ME WHEN SHE BADE ME GOOD-BYE AND SENT ME TO YOU.
WHAT DO YOU WISH ME TO DO?
SEND ME BACK TO KANSAS WHERE MY AUNT EM AND UNCLE HENRY ARE.
I DON'T LIKE YOUR COUNTRY, ALTHOUGH IT'S SO BEAUTIFUL.
AND I'M SURE AUNT EM WILL BE DREADFULLY WORRIED OVER MY BEING AWAY SO LONG.

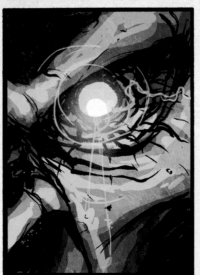

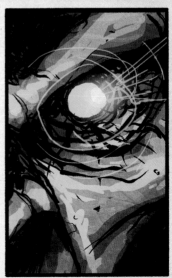

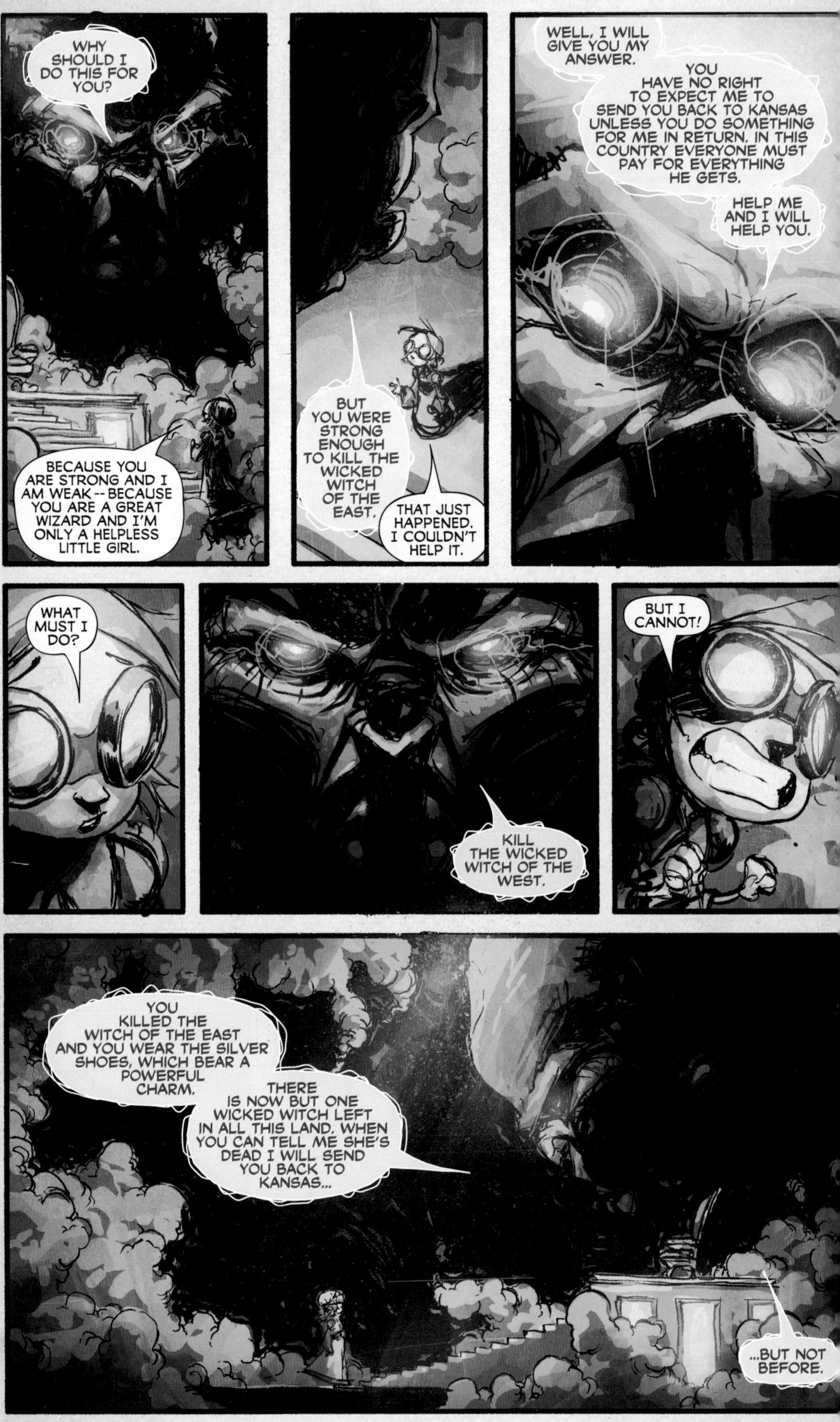
WHY SHOULD I DO THIS FOR YOU?
BECAUSE YOU ARE STRONG AND I AM WEAK -- BECAUSE YOU ARE A GREAT WIZARD AND I'M ONLY A HELPLESS LITTLE GIRL.
BUT YOU WERE STRONG ENOUGH TO KILL THE WICKED WITCH OF THE EAST.
THAT JUST HAPPENED. I COULDN'T HELP IT.
WELL, I WILL GIVE YOU MY ANSWER.
YOU HAVE NO RIGHT TO EXPECT ME TO SEND YOU BACK TO KANSAS UNLESS YOU DO SOMETHING FOR ME IN RETURN. IN THIS COUNTRY EVERYONE MUST PAY FOR EVERYTHING HE GETS.
HELP ME AND I WILL HELP YOU.
WHAT MUST I DO?
KILL THE WICKED WITCH OF THE WEST.
BUT I CANNOT!
YOU KILLED THE WITCH OF THE EAST AND YOU WEAR THE SILVER SHOES, WHICH BEAR A POWERFUL CHARM.
THERE IS NOW BUT ONE WICKED WITCH LEFT IN ALL THIS LAND. WHEN YOU CAN TELL ME SHE'S DEAD I WILL SEND YOU BACK TO KANSAS...
...BUT NOT BEFORE.

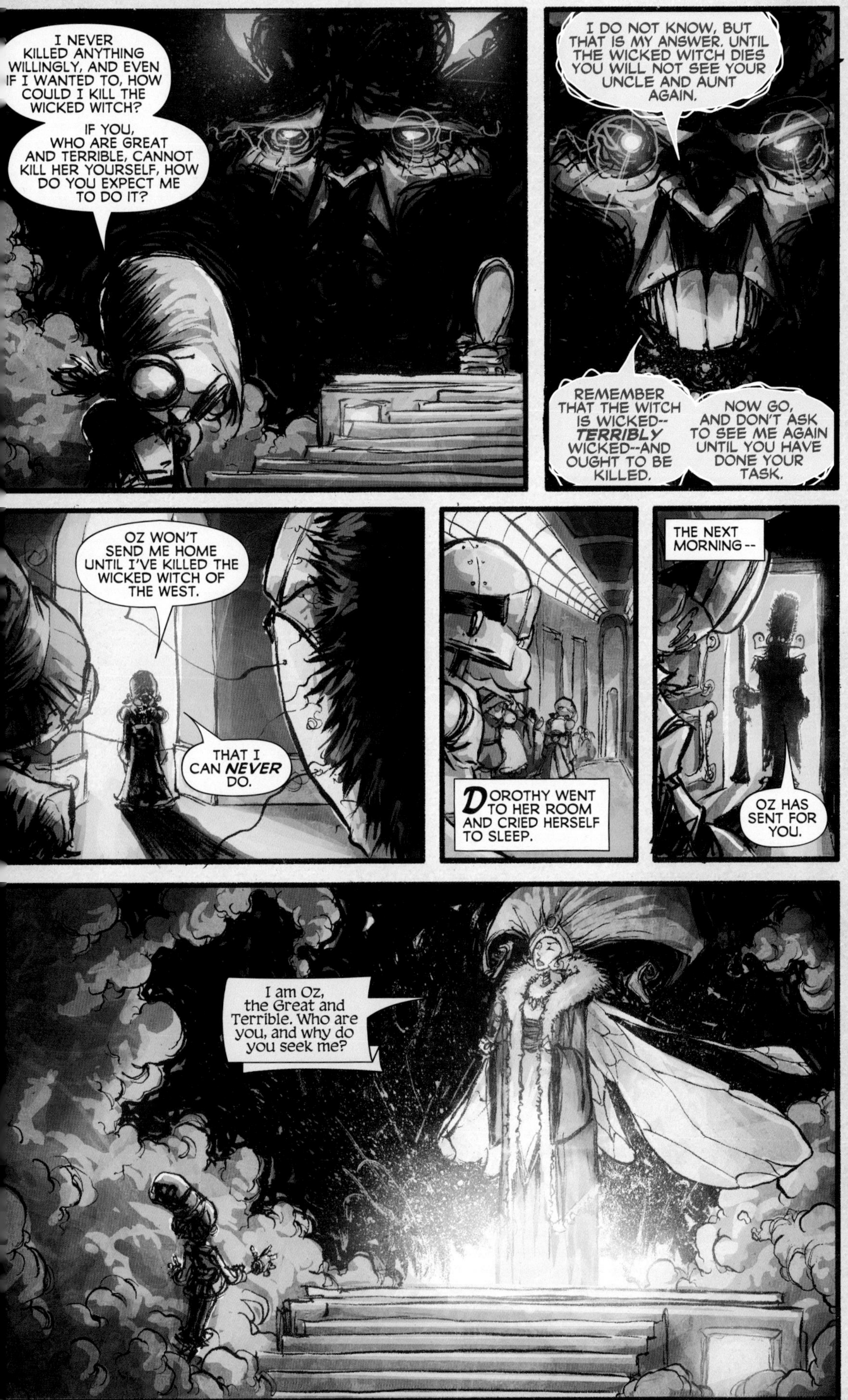

I NEVER KILLED ANYTHING WILLINGLY, AND EVEN IF I WANTED TO, HOW COULD I KILL THE WICKED WITCH?
IF YOU, WHO ARE GREAT AND TERRIBLE, CANNOT KILL HER YOURSELF, HOW DO YOU EXPECT ME TO DO IT?
I DO NOT KNOW, BUT THAT IS MY ANSWER. UNTIL THE WICKED WITCH DIES YOU WILL NOT SEE YOUR UNCLE AND AUNT AGAIN.
REMEMBER THAT THE WITCH IS WICKED--TERRIBLY WICKED--AND OUGHT TO BE KILLED.
NOW GO, AND DON'T ASK TO SEE ME AGAIN UNTIL YOU HAVE DONE YOUR TASK.
OZ WON'T SEND ME HOME UNTIL I'VE KILLED THE WICKED WITCH OF THE WEST.
THAT I CAN NEVER DO.
DOROTHY WENT TO HER ROOM AND CRIED HERSELF TO SLEEP.
THE NEXT MORNING--
OZ HAS SENT FOR YOU.
I am Oz, the Great and Terrible. Who are you, and why do you seek me?

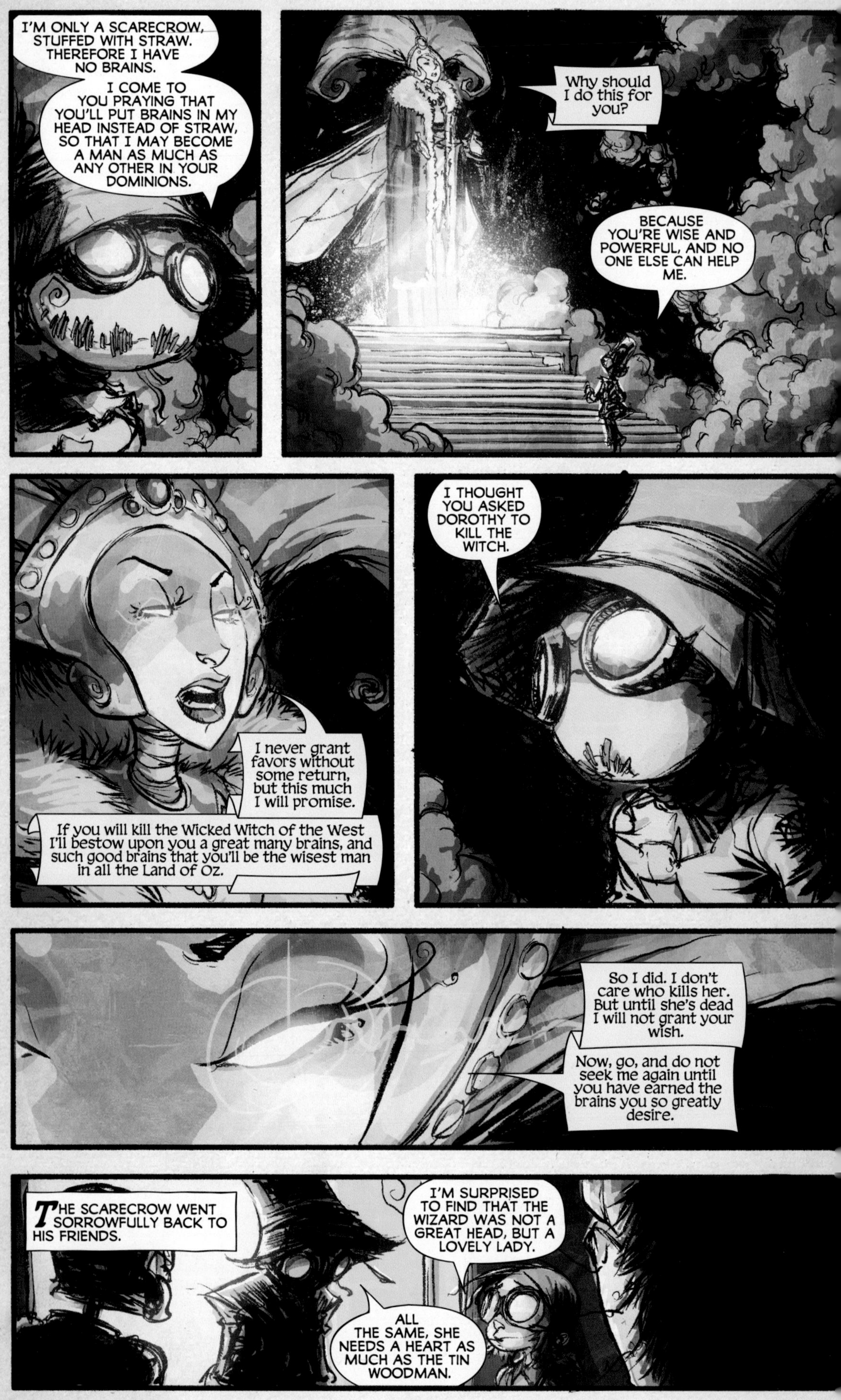
I'M ONLY A SCARECROW, STUFFED WITH STRAW. THEREFORE I HAVE NO BRAINS.
I COME TO YOU PRAYING THAT YOU'LL PUT BRAINS IN MY HEAD INSTEAD OF STRAW, SO THAT I MAY BECOME A MAN AS MUCH AS ANY OTHER IN YOUR DOMINIONS.
Why should I do this for you?
BECAUSE YOU'RE WISE AND POWERFUL, AND NO ONE ELSE CAN HELP ME.
I never grant favors without some return, but this much I will promise.
If you will kill the Wicked Witch of the West I'll bestow upon you a great many brains, and such good brains that you'll be the wisest man in all the Land of Oz.
I THOUGHT YOU ASKED DOROTHY TO KILL THE WITCH.
So I did. I don't care who kills her. But until she's dead I will not grant your wish.
Now, go, and do not seek me again until you have earned the brains you so greatly desire.
THE SCARECROW WENT SORROWFULLY BACK TO HIS FRIENDS.
I'M SURPRISED TO FIND THAT THE WIZARD WAS NOT A GREAT HEAD, BUT A LOVELY LADY.
ALL THE SAME, SHE NEEDS A HEART AS MUCH AS THE TIN WOODMAN.

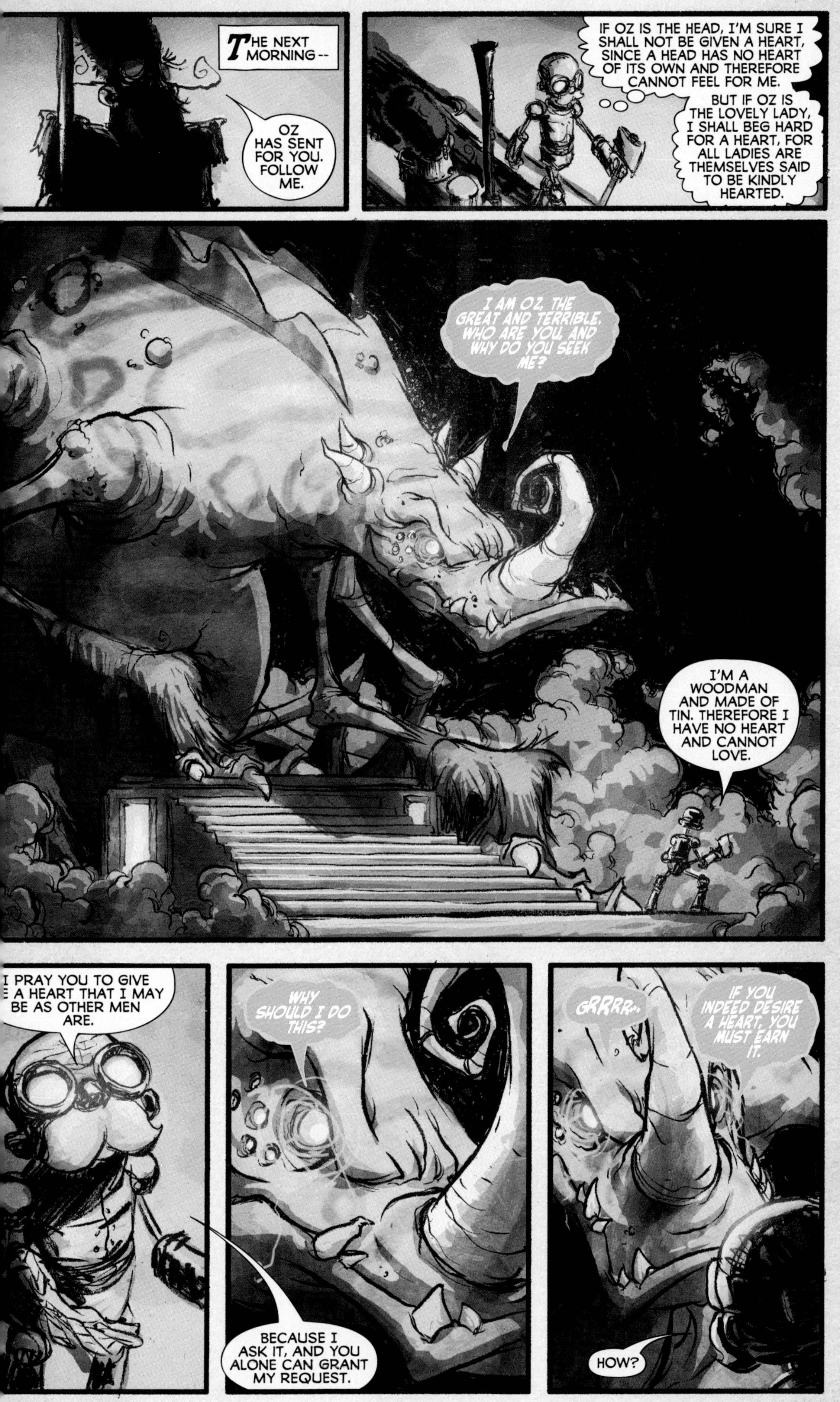
THE NEXT MORNING--
OZ HAS SENT FOR YOU. FOLLOW ME.
IF OZ IS THE HEAD, I'M SURE I SHALL NOT BE GIVEN A HEART, SINCE A HEAD HAS NO HEART OF ITS OWN AND THEREFORE CANNOT FEEL FOR ME.
BUT IF OZ IS THE LOVELY LADY, I SHALL BEG HARD FOR A HEART, FOR ALL LADIES ARE THEMSELVES SAID TO BE KINDLY HEARTED.
I AM OZ, THE GREAT AND TERRIBLE. WHO ARE YOU, AND WHY DO YOU SEEK ME?
I'M A WOODMAN AND MADE OF TIN. THEREFORE I HAVE NO HEART AND CANNOT LOVE.
I PRAY YOU TO GIVE E A HEART THAT I MAY BE AS OTHER MEN ARE.
WHY SHOULD I DO THIS?
BECAUSE I ASK IT, AND YOU ALONE CAN GRANT MY REQUEST.
GRRRR..
IF YOU INDEED DESIRE A HEART, YOU MUST EARN IT.
HOW?

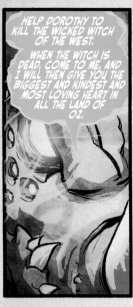

HELP DOROTHY TO KILL THE WICKED WITCH OF THE WEST.

WHEN THE WITCH IS DEAD, COME TO ME, AND I WILL THEN GIVE YOU THE BIGGEST AND KINDEST AND MOST LOVING HEART IN ALL THE LAND OF OZ.

*T*HE TIN WOODMAN WAS FORCED TO RETURN SORROWFULLY TO HIS FRIENDS.

IF HE'S A BEAST WHEN *I* GO TO SEE HIM, I SHALL ROAR MY LOUDEST, AND SO FRIGHTEN HIM THAT HE WILL GRANT ALL I ASK.

AND IF HE'S THE LOVELY LADY, I SHALL PRETEND TO SPRING UPON HER, AND SO COMPEL HER TO DO MY BIDDING.

AND IF HE'S THE GREAT HEAD, HE'LL BE AT MY MERCY, FO I'LL ROLL THIS HEAD ALL ABOUT THE ROO. UNTIL HE PROMISES TO GIVE US WHAT WE DESIRE.

SO BE OF GOOD CHEER, MY FRIENDS, FOR ALL WILL YET BE WELL.

*T*HE NEXT MORNING --

THE LION'S FIRST THOUGHT WAS THAT OZ HAD BY ACCIDENT CAUGHT ON FIRE AND WAS BURNING UP. BUT WHEN HE TRIED TO GO NEARER THE HEAT SINGED HIS WHISKERS.

I am Oz, the Great and Terrible. Who are you, and why do you seek me?

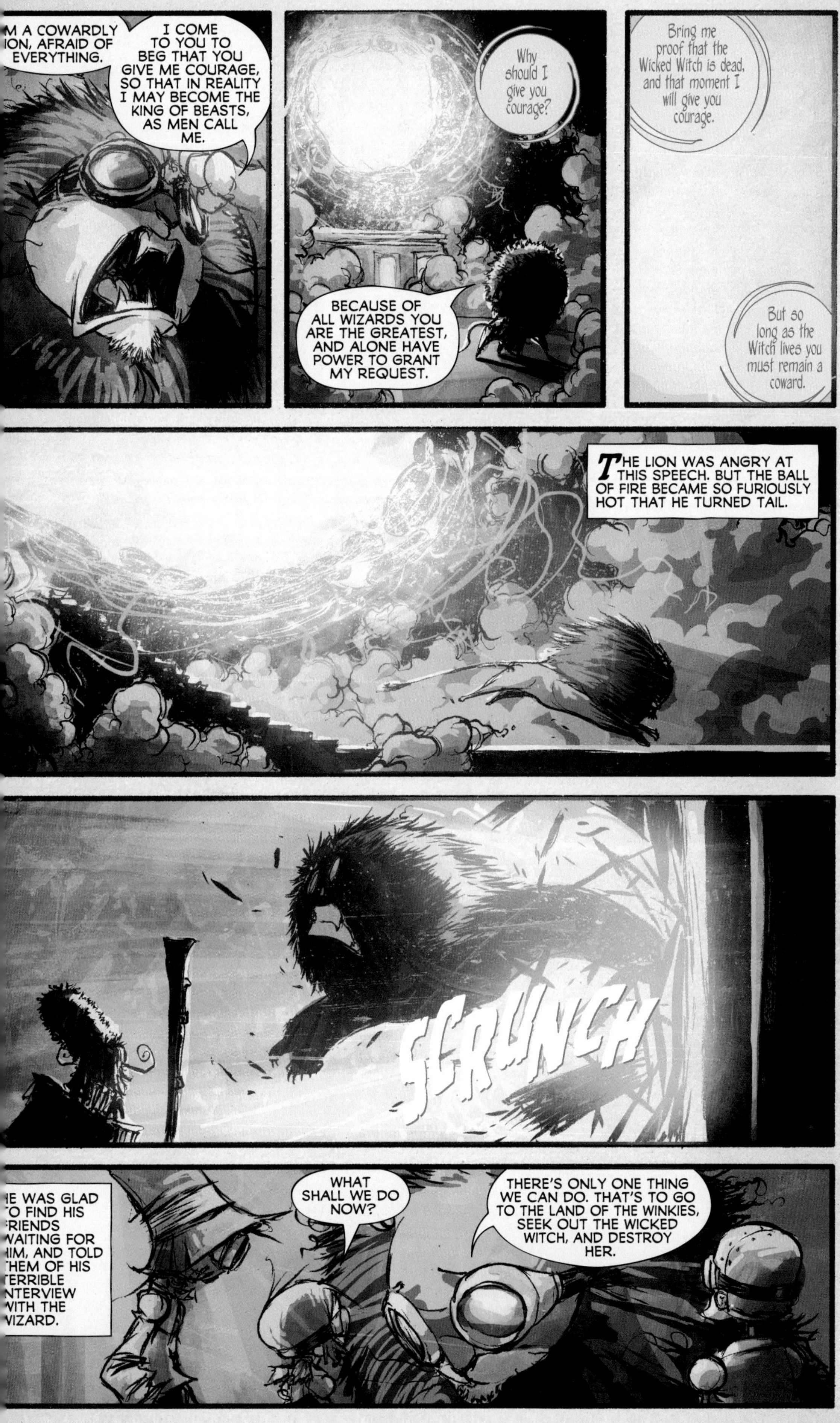
M A COWARDLY
ION, AFRAID OF
EVERYTHING.
I COME TO YOU TO BEG THAT YOU GIVE ME COURAGE, SO THAT IN REALITY I MAY BECOME THE KING OF BEASTS, AS MEN CALL ME.
Why should I give you courage?
BECAUSE OF ALL WIZARDS YOU ARE THE GREATEST, AND ALONE HAVE POWER TO GRANT MY REQUEST.
Bring me proof that the Wicked Witch is dead, and that moment I will give you courage.
But so long as the Witch lives you must remain a coward.
THE LION WAS ANGRY AT THIS SPEECH. BUT THE BALL OF FIRE BECAME SO FURIOUSLY HOT THAT HE TURNED TAIL.
SCRUNCH
IE WAS GLAD TO FIND HIS FRIENDS WAITING FOR HIM, AND TOLD THEM OF HIS TERRIBLE INTERVIEW WITH THE WIZARD.
WHAT SHALL WE DO NOW?
THERE'S ONLY ONE THING WE CAN DO. THAT'S TO GO TO THE LAND OF THE WINKIES, SEEK OUT THE WICKED WITCH, AND DESTROY HER.

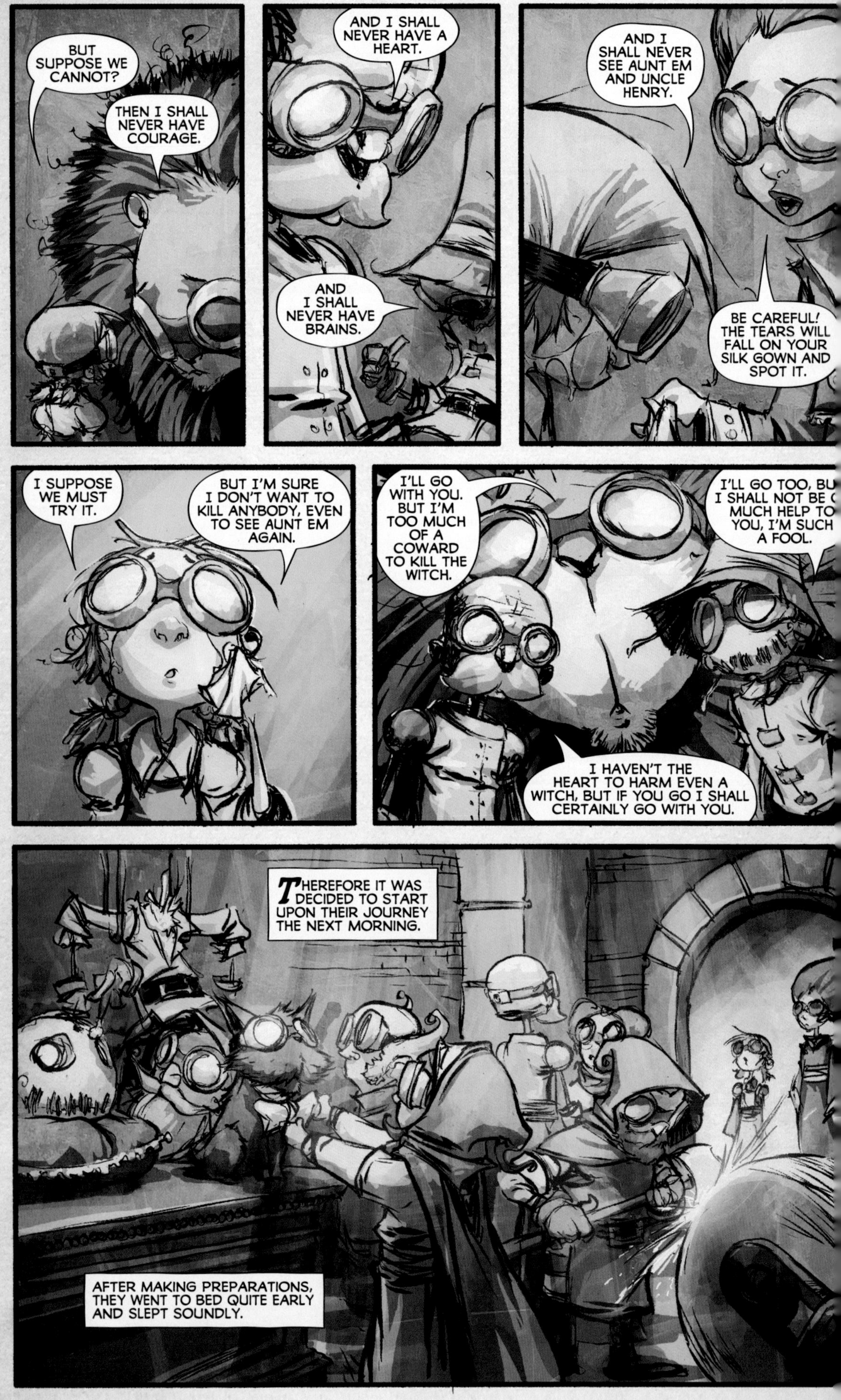
BUT SUPPOSE WE CANNOT?
THEN I SHALL NEVER HAVE COURAGE.
AND I SHALL NEVER HAVE A HEART.
AND I SHALL NEVER HAVE BRAINS.
AND I SHALL NEVER SEE AUNT EM AND UNCLE HENRY.
BE CAREFUL! THE TEARS WILL FALL ON YOUR SILK GOWN AND SPOT IT.
I SUPPOSE WE MUST TRY IT.
BUT I'M SURE I DON'T WANT TO KILL ANYBODY, EVEN TO SEE AUNT EM AGAIN.
I'LL GO WITH YOU. BUT I'M TOO MUCH OF A COWARD TO KILL THE WITCH.
I'LL GO TOO, BU I SHALL NOT BE MUCH HELP TO YOU, I'M SUCH A FOOL.
I HAVEN'T THE HEART TO HARM EVEN A WITCH, BUT IF YOU GO I SHALL CERTAINLY GO WITH YOU.
THEREFORE IT WAS DECIDED TO START UPON THEIR JOURNEY THE NEXT MORNING.
AFTER MAKING PREPARATIONS, THEY WENT TO BED QUITE EARLY AND SLEPT SOUNDLY.